THE UNEXPURGATED ADVENTURES OF

SHERLOCK HOLMES

BOOK 9

THE ADVENTURE OF THE ENGINEER'S TONGUE

by NP Sercombe

The un-edited manuscript originally entitled *The Adventure of the Engineer's Thumb* written by Dr. John Watson and Sir Arthur Conan Doyle

Illustrations by Juliet Snape

EVA Books

This novel is entirely a work of fiction. The names, characters and incidents portrayed in it are the work of the author's and illustrator's imaginations. Any resemblance to actual persons, living or dead, events or localities, is entirely coincidental.

Published by EVA BOOKS 2020 – c/o Harry King Films Limited
1&2 The Barn
West Stoke Road
Lavant
n/r Chichester
West Sussex PO18 9AA

A CIP catalogue record for this book is available from the British Library.

ISBN 978-1-9996961-8-4 (Hardback)

Book layout & cover design by Clare Brayshaw.

Cover illustration by Juliet Snape.

Set in Bruce Old Style.

Prepared and printed by: York Publishing Services Ltd
64 Hallfield Road, Layerthorpe, York YO31 7ZQ

Tel: 01904 431213

Website: www.yps-publishing.co.uk

THE UNEXPURGATED ADVENTURES OF SHERLOCK HOLMES

Books in the Series:

A BALLS-UP IN BOHEMIA
THE MYSTERIOUS CASE OF MR. GINGERNUTS
THE CASE OF THE RANDY STEPFATHER
MY FIRST PROPER RURAL MURDER
THE ORANGES OF DEATH!
THE MAN WITH THE HAIRY FACE
A GANDER AT THE BLUE CARBUNCLE
THE SPECKLED BAND SPECULATION
THE ADVENTURE OF THE ENGINEER'S TONGUE

Nicholas Sercombe is a writer and producer for film and television. He has been lucky enough to work in comedy for most of the Holocene period with some of the greatest performers and writers. He is most comfortable when reading Conan Doyle and even happier when re-writing these extraordinarily entertaining stories by Dr. John Watson.

Juliet Snape studied illustration at Cambridge School of Art and Central St. Martins. She has illustrated over 100 books and her work has been published around the world.

She is a fan of Sherlock Holmes – her father even lived in Baker Street – and, in the words of Conan Doyle, she is *"naturally gravitated to London, that great cesspool into which all the loungers and idlers of the Empire are irresistibly drained."* She lives in London and loves sketching, finding inspiration all around her. She has two children, both successful creatives.

For lovers of horseracing at Ascot

The Adventure of the Engineer's Tongue

(published in The Strand in March 1892 as
THE ADVENTURE OF THE ENGINEER'S THUMB
by Dr. Watson and Arthur Conan Doyle)

It was the glorious summer of 1890. Holmes and I had attended Ascot races. We had been invited to stay down in Berkshire, as privileged guests of the Earl of Coventry, the Master of Buckhounds, the Queen's representative at Ascot (because Ma'am never showed up) and a client of Mr. Sherlock Holmes. The Earl had been relieved of an obnoxious extortionist by the great detective and he was keen to show his gratitude by including us in his perennial house party where for three days, and what seemed like five nights, we attended the most sociable sporting fixture in the social calendar. He had taken a house in Sunninghill and filled it with fellow nobility, fashionable do-gooders of the day and...us. We were not the only commoners; there was also a trainer or two in residence, the ones that knew how to doff their caps, even if they had been sent to the right school.

I had presumed that Holmes and I would be *homines in hostem* – fishes out of water gasping for survival on the riverbank – but nothing could be further from the truth. When we settled in for luncheon on Monday morning – the day of our arrival – we became the immediate attraction of conversation in the dining salon. Naturally, the great detective declared his reputation being brought to the fore by word-of-mouth, not the occasional newspaper headline about his successful outcomes, or, in the main, due to my accounts published in the *The Strand* magazine, which was now selling like hot cakes. It was due to the sale of over a half a million copies per issue that the party was well-acquainted with the details of our adventures and thanks to the editing process inflicted on my manuscripts by George Newnes, Holmes and I appeared to be two angelic knights-in-shining-armour, pure-of-heart, noble-in-spirit, upholding Christian values, devoted to a life of valour in the fight against evil-doers, solving unsolvable mysteries and saving innocent souls. It was also thanks to the censorship that they were blissfully unaware of our somewhat sardonic approach to our clients, our wayward social activities and the ravaging of fallen women. Perfect! This was *the* moment when we knew that Sherlock Holmes and his trusty companion, Dr. Watson, had a foothold in British Society. We enjoyed our moment in the limelight, but little did we know that even more unsolicited fame was on its way.

The next morning was the first day of Ascot Races, which was the dawn of a new civilisation for me. I had been racing on numerous occasions but never to this elite gathering of English and Irish Society. The Ascot Meet is not for the plebeian it is where the great and the good take stock of the finest thoroughbreds in the land – i.e. of one another – and gamble on horseracing as if there is no tomorrow. This was the beating heart of fashionable society, where the peacocks displayed their wealth and peahens their suitability. Everyone was dressed in their finest splendour.

I may have been an Ascot virgin but this equine *rendez-vous* was an annual pilgrimage for Sherlock Holmes. He was as relaxed as I had ever seen him; comfortable in this most aristocratic environment, nodding a head at almost every turn. In army terms: he knew some nobs; the nobs knew him. Strange, I thought, for the son of a physicist and a botanist. I was not sure how this had come about. Maybe it was all connected to his *alma mater*, which was…? Now there was a thought: just where did Holmes go to school? He had never mentioned it. I made a mental note to ask him.

Being house guests of Lord Coventry, we were ensconced in the royal enclosure, which was a grand title for a tiered, two-storey viewing building not unlike the one at Surbiton railway station. But it was situated on the finish line, and it was the only place to be. His lordship's horse, The Deemster, a great big ball of muscle directly descended from The Brierly Turk, turned out to be the fastest animal on the course that day. Even so, he was not as fast as Sherlock Holmes extracting all of the notes from my wallet and placing it on the great big ball of gristle that came plum last, wheezing its way over the line.

'Holmes,' said I, exasperated, as The Deemster strutted his stuff in front of our host by the winner's post. 'Why on Earth did you risk all of our money on Dinsmore Nuisance?'

'Because, dear Doctor, the hopeless Dinsmore Nuisance is trained by Colonel Blanders, one of our fellow house guests, who told me at last night's dinner table that his charge could not, and would not, lose the race.'

'Clearly, this Colonel Blanders chap must be in love with Dinsmore Nuisance.'

'And love is blind, Doctor? Is that what you are saying?'

'Yes, Holmes, I am! We could not see that the animal was a wobbler but Colonel Blanders should have done. He is obviously a fool and, certainly, he cannot be trusted. I shall be having words with him later on.'

But I did better than just to confront the chap. Later, that evening, Lord Coventry entertained two hundred of his closest friends for a celebration of his fine victory. It was a gathering of the very noblest gentry. During early evening snifters, I slipped up behind the pinch-faced Blanders, who looked like a chap who could be bad-tempered, whilst he was leering at a young lady on the far side of the room. I spiked his cocktail with a small pipette of phenolphthalein, a vigorous laxative that I kept in my medical bag. Then, I settled down to enjoy myself. First, I asked him, tongue-in-cheek, if he had shot his useless horse. By God, he had! Anyway, I continued to engage him in banal conversation – frankly, it was fabricated gossip and all that he was capable of (and he was a foreigner of some sort) – and sure enough, a few minutes later the powerful loosener started to permeate his insides. He looked distracted, eyes bobbing side to side. Then, he became nervous, and shifted from foot to foot. But I wouldn't let him go; all part of the game. He jawed on and I tempted him with some more juicy morsels of claptrap. Suddenly his face shattered, like a cheap mirror, and he ran for the door, taking no prisoners, ladies and gentlemen being barged out of his way recklessly. It was hilarious! To cap it all, somebody in the throng of elegance shouted out "I say, he's much faster than his horse, what?" which brought the house down! Clearly, Colonel Blanders was not a popular man and, thankfully, that was the last we saw of him.

Day Two of Ascot was an early start. We were obliged to be *in situ* at "Surbiton Central" before His Royal Highness, The Prince of Wales, made an appearance. We experienced a tedious carriage ride in the pouring rain, the excellent footmen attending us meticulously, raising the roof in a trice during a downpour a mile or so from the racecourse. But it was the half-crown tip that was a stab in the Ascot week treasure chest – yes, dear reader, we were down to coins only, so the chances of a restoration of our fortunes lay in the backing of a massive outsider. This would be a minor miracle but, as any follower of the turf will tell you, it ain't over until The Getting Out Stakes has been run.

It was around noon that the royal enclosure was graced by HRH Bertie The Bounder. It was the first time that I had clapped eyes upon him. He was larger than life, weighing in at about eighteen stone, and louder than an elephant as he trumpeted greetings to friends and acquaintances. I am told that on this day he was at his most rumbustious, all laughter and guffaws of bonhomie as his introductions fell all over the place, fawning and sucking up to him. When it was our turn, I stood bolt upright, to attention, army-style upon imminent presentation of royalty. Lord Coventry introduced Sherlock Holmes first. He stood straight enough – for a civvy, I suppose – and inclined his head a tad when taking the prince's hand but I would say that he looked down his nose a little. The prince was polite enough to acknowledge Holmes as someone he heard of. Then, it was my turn, and he lit up.

‘Ohhh!! You are Mr. Holmes’s fag!’ exclaimed the royal barrelage, and I nodded and smiled as everybody nearby fell about laughing.

‘Sir, I am fagged out looking after him!’ said I, with bluff repartee.

The fat prince clapped his hands to his sides and laughed himself puce. ‘You can be *my* fag instead!’ he bellowed. ‘Call me Bertie! Now come along here, my dear chap. Be by my side. Shoo, Mister Holmes! Moosh! You go off and do some detecting, there’s a good fellow!”

Holmes blanched, and was taken aback. I gave him a withering look, accompanied by a rippling dismissal of the fingers. ‘Moosh!’ I hissed. “Moosh!’ Slowly, Holmes retreated, poteen-resentful but proud – my order was, after all, by royal command. That would teach him to be aloof to royalty.

So, as Bertie’s fag, I was now employed as his sergeant-at-arms, which involved being his pimp to fetch pretty girls, his secretary to notate his private wagers and his dummy to execute his incessant jokes, some of which were very funny. I found Bertie to be a very amusing man with a spellbinding charisma. For instance, every time he wanted me to run an errand he would shout ‘FAG!’ and I would have to abandon my activities, run across the room and present myself instantly, to attention, for his instructions, entertaining his toadies, causing much hilarity. By three o’clock he was full to the brim with fine liquor and had turned into a Bohemian lunatic living his last day on the planet, like a mad bear running amok in the woods in the heat of the mating season, a licence to thrill and be thrilled, touching gentlemen’s wallets and ladies’ parts in a whirlwind of bad behaviour. A couple of years have gone by now but, on reflection, I suppose he was at his apogee of Society excess, only just a few weeks before the royal baccarat scandal, the public exposure from which he never recovered his maximum ebullience until he became king. It was during this latter half of the afternoon that we bumped into the diminutive and walrus-whiskered, Prince Soltykoff.

'Ah, Saltycock!' hailed Bertie, which forced the Russian nobleman to leave off fussing about a chair with a female companion and to turn his attention – walrus whiskers met the walrus of love. 'Yes, there you are! I was making a bee-line for you! I hear that your horse has a decent chance in the Gold Cup tomorrow, what?'

'Your highness...' said the prince, inclining his head only a nod, on the same social level of one prince to another, 'that is why I named him "Gold."'

'I don't quite follow, old chap?'

'"Gold" is Pure Gold in the Gold Cup! That will be the headline in the Chronicle* this Friday.'

'Well, you should ruddy well know!' said Bertie. He referred to the fact that Soltykoff owned the newspaper. 'But he must win the race first. He's a dead-certainty, eh?'

'He had that little stumble in the Chester trial,' reported the prince, pulling Bertie into a boys-own whisper, 'so, as luck would have it, he is fourteen pounds in hand for this race. That's four lengths on the field.' He tapped the side of his nose knowingly.

* *The Jewish Chronicle*

'You rascal, you!' Bertie clapped the little chap on the shoulder and they laughed their socks off. But then he stopped dead – his eyes had caught sight of his friend's female companion, who had raised herself up from her seat. She turned around to face him.

'And a *very* good afternoon to you madame! ' said Bertie agog, with a face like a leaping salmon. 'Look lively, Saltycock!'

'Your highness, may I present to you Mrs. Charlotte Hudson...'

Yes, dear readers, it was our landlady! I have to say that she scrubbed up beautifully, looking fabulous in a finely tailored summer dress, large floral print on white cotton with coral piping, drawn in tight about the waist and from there a cascading bluebell down to the hem, topped and tailed with a white sombrero-style hat and leather ankle boots to match. For a lady that must be in her mid-thirties – and I am only guessing – she stood out like a golden statuette in Surbiton Central that afternoon. Bertie proffered his royal mitt. She took it and dipped a curtsey with the graceful elegance of a swan. He drew her hand towards him and slobbered all over her glove.

'And Mister Hudson?'

'He went west.'

'My commiserations!' remarked he, without a shred of remorse.

'It was meant to be,' said she, placing her forefinger on her lower lip, tilting her head to one side and flashing me a glance with a look that told me I cut more than a dash in my morning coat than I thought, but said also: "Don't you say a thing!"

'FAG!', shouted Bertie, making me an introduction to Mrs. Hudson before taking me to one side. He whispered into my ear, instructing me to place bets with his noblemen friends that I had been introduced to during the day.

'Now, remember, young fellow,' said he in a summing-up way, 'the name of Saltycock's horse is "Gold." So, remember, it is Gold to win the Gold Cup tomorrow, yes?'

I nodded.

'Don't take less than seven-to-one and don't spend more than twenty-five.'

'Yes, sir! No less than seven-to-one.'

'Good fag!'

'And no more than twenty-five guineas.'

'Bad Fag! No, it is seven-to-one and twenty-five *thousand* guineas.' His orders delivered, he turned around to slobber all over our landlady again, leaving me stunned at the thought of representing such a massive gamble.

'Mrs. Hudson,' he continued, 'we shall watch this renewal of the Hunt Cup entwined. Come along now – hop on board!'

Bertie extended his arm to Mrs. Hudson. She cocked him an eye and feigned a poor aim, the tease, hooking it with a colourful smile that tickled old Bertie pink. As they ambled their way to the royal box, she gave me a catnip wink and an audacious lick of her top lip. After my most recent afternoon of intercourse with Charlotte Hudson*, in which she seduced my flagship to crash

---

* see *The A Gander at the Blue Carbuncle*

artfully onto the rocks four times in one afternoon, I knew what Bertie was in for. He may have had a tall reputation as a champion sailor, but I wondered if his *fo'c'sle* would withstand the relentless onslaught of Mrs Hudson's cruel sea.

* * *

That Thursday morning, a little before six o'clock, I was awakened by the maid tapping at the bedroom door, to announce that a man had come from Prince Soltykoff's and was asking for me. She told me that the man had hurt himself and that it was urgent. I thought that something dastardly must be afoot to be knocked up at this time of the day, and so I dressed hurriedly. As I descended the staircase, I was surprised about how healthy I was feeling after such a lively day as The Prince of Wales's runner and an evening of watching Sherlock Holmes bag about a hundred pounds playing bridge, thus redeeming our fund for gambling. I was met by Lord Coventry's head butler, Sandy – a tall man and ex-military – who greeted me in his rather individual style.

'Sorry to tear you away from your warm bed, you lovely doctor, you!' chirruped he, all of a twitter, and camp as a row of tents. 'But this nice man who's come to see you, well, he's in a bit of a state! Oh, and he is bleeding *ev-e-ry-where*! Bleeding like a stuck pig! Sooo... I just couldn't have him staining all of these nice rugs, could I? I had to put him into my little hidey-hole. Walk this way...'

Sandy minced off and I followed, thinking that if I was to walk that way I'd be dancing Odette in Swan Lake this evening. As we headed towards the domestic

His Royal Highness drank in the stunning Mrs Hudson like she was a fine Montrachet.

side of the house I wondered just why so many army and navy folk were named Sandy? To me, it was one of life's great conundrums. Anyway, this Sandy was known by all and sundry, staff and guests alike, as "Dandy Sandy."

We descended deeper into the building via a back staircase and walked along a couple of passages. He stopped me by a door, which was ajar, adequate for me to see into a bright parlour that was all white ceramic tiles, pine cupboards and bleached oak wooden floor. He prodded my shoulder with his long, slender forefinger and leaned in close – within a hair's breadth – to my ear.

'Now! Just a word of warning, Doctor... When I left him he was in a little bit of a fluster about his injury. But I sat him down. I told him that I had sent for you. I gave him a shoulder massage. He seemed to calm down. He's quite a big man. You know... quite butch. Hmmm! On a good day, I'd say he's quite a dish!'

'Yes, calm down, Sandy. Thank you. Now let's take a look at him.'

I pushed the door and we walked into the room. There, sitting at the table, was Dandy Sandy's fancy and, on first sight, I could appreciate what excited him so. He was a very handsome man of about five-and-twenty years, quietly dressed in a suit of heather tweed, with a soft cloth cap, which he had laid down upon the table-top. He had a strong masculine face, with a moustache, naturally, but he was exceedingly pale and gave me the impression of a man who was suffering from some agitation, which it took all his strength of mind to control. Then I noticed that round one of his hands he had a handkerchief wrapped that was saturated with blood and dripping onto the floor.

'I am sorry to knock you up so early, Doctor,' said he, with a very heavy lisp in his speech, which was an alarmingly distraction, 'but I have had a very serious accident during the night. I came by Sunningdale to the Soltykoff residence by sheer chance. It was one of the house guests, a certain Mrs. Hudson, who recommended you as a worthy fellow and I was driven here in great haste by one of the gardeners. Upon arrival I gave the butler my card.'

I decided not to enquire about his speech impediment, which I presumed to be a defect from birth, although I noticed some dried blood splattered upon his starched collar. Hmmm! Anyway, I took the card and read it out loud, saving my new patient the effort. 'Mr. Victor Hatherley, hydraulic engineer, 16a Victoria Street (3rd Floor),' said I, sitting down in the chair opposite. 'I regret that I have kept you waiting. You are fresh from a journey, I understand, and have experienced a calamitous night?'

'Oh, to call my night calamitous would be a massive understatement!' cried he. Then, he laughed heartily. But he laughed without interruption, and for ages, with an ascending scale of tone, up to a very high ringing note, leaning back in his chair and shaking his sides. Together with more dried blood stains on his neck it was a chillingly horrible atmosphere, and he just wouldn't finish! All my medical instincts rose up against that laugh: the man was in shock and hysterical.

'STOP IT!' I cried. 'Pull yourself together!' and I poured out some water from a carafe and glanced at the servant hovering. 'Bring some brandy, Dandy! Sorry, I mean... Sandy! Quickly now!'

The butler nodded acknowledgment and left the room. Mr. Hatherley was laughing and crying at the same time, one of those hysterical outbursts which come upon a strong character when some great crisis is over and gone. Presently he came to himself once more, very weary, and blushing hotly and with tears in his eyes.

'I am sorry. I have been making a fool of myself,' he gasped, just as Dandy Sandy deposited a decanter and two small balloons. Separately, he laid out carbolic acid, iodine, liniment, bandages, hot water and some neat alcohol. This butler chap was a resourceful fellow and I nodded my appreciation.

'Not at all. Drink this!' I dashed some brandy into the water. He drank, wincing feverishly, and the colour began to come back to his bloodless cheeks. 'And some of this!' Mr. Hatherley drank from the bottle of neat alcohol, went bright red in the face, screamed, and coughed uncontrollably, rolling around in his wooden chair. Eventually, he took back control.

'Jesus Christ! ' said he, regaining his composure. 'That's better! And now, Doctor, perhaps you would kindly attend to my thumb, or rather the place where my thumb used to be.'

He took another slug of brandy and unwound the handkerchief. He held out his hand. I have to tell you, dear adventure enthusiasts, that the sight gave even my hardened nerves a shudder to look at it. There were four protruding fingers and a horrid red spongy surface where the thumb should have been. It had been hacked or torn out from the roots. Behind us there was a heavy thump! as Dandy Sandy fainted unconscious onto the floor.

'Good heavens!' I cried. 'This is a terrible injury! It must have bled considerably.'

'Good morning, Wilkie Collins! Too bloody right it did! I fainted when it was done; and I think that I must have been senseless for a long time. When I came to, I found that it was still bleeding, so I tied one end of my handkerchief very tightly round the wrist and braced it up with a twig.'

'Excellent! You should have been a surgeon.'

'It is a question of hydraulics, you see. It came within my own province.'

'This has been done,' said I examining the wound, 'by a very heavy and sharp instrument.'

'A thing like a cleaver,' said he.

'An accident, I presume?'

'By no means!'

'What, a murderous attack?'

'Very murderous indeed!'

'You horrify me.'

I sponged the wound, cleaned it, dressed it; and, finally, covered it with cotton wadding and carbolised bandages. He lay back without wincing, though he bit his lip from time to time.

'How is that?' I asked, when I had finished.

'Capital! Between your brandy, that transparent stuff, whatever that was, and your bandage, I feel a new man. I was very weak, but I have had a good deal to go through.'

'Perhaps you had better not speak of the matter. It is evidently playing on your nerves and you seem to have a speech impediment. Can you tell me if you have always had such a profound and awkward lisp?'

'Oh, no, Doctor, not now! This is very much part of my tale, which I shall have to tell to the police; but, between ourselves, if it were not for the convincing evidence of my thumb wound and the cause of my speech impediment, I should be surprised if they believed my statement, for it is a very extraordinary story, and I have not much in the way of proof with which to back it up. And, even if they believe me, the clues which I can give them are so vague that it is a question whether justice will be done.'

'Ha!' cried I, 'if it is anything in the nature of a problem which you desire to see solved, I should strongly recommend you come to my friend Sherlock Holmes before you go to the official police.'

Oh, I have heard of that fellow,' answered my patient.

'Well, my friend, you are in luck. I am Doctor Watson!'

He stared at me, vacantly. 'Yes, and I am very pleased to meet you, Doctor.' He blinked. He had no recognition of my name whatsoever. Huh! Clearly, he was too ignorant to read *The Strand*. I said nothing and let him stew.

'Anyway,' says he, 'I should be very glad if this Sherlock Holmes would take the matter up, though of course I must use the official police as well. Would you be able to give me an introduction to him?'

'I can do better. I can take you to him myself right now!'

'I should be immensely obliged to you.'

'He is here already. Let me rouse this haemophobic butler,' said I, reaching into my pocket for my bottle of smelling-salts, 'and we shall breakfast together.'

* * *

Sherlock Holmes was sitting in the south wing library in his dressing-gown, reading the agony column of *The Times*, and smoking his before-breakfast pipe, which was composed of all the plugs and dottles left from his smokes the day before, all carefully dried and collected on the corner of the mantelpiece, a vulgar habit that he continued to practice even in other person's homes. He received us in his quietly genial fashion, ordered fresh rashers and eggs, and we placed our own requests. Sandy arranged for a footman to set up a table especially for us, away from the other house guests, so that we may have a private conference. Not much was said before and during our hearty meal, for as soon as Holmes learned about Mr. Hatherley's acute lisp, he indicated to me that in preference to him talking we should let him eat, because it was obvious to both of us that he was in considerable pain when masticating. There was also competition – the distraction of the changing weather outside where a huge thunderstorm approached. There were boulders of black clouds mantling the landscape and rolling toward us across the cricket square; as the bright June morning sunshine was engulfed, the room became darker and darker and I began to feel a sense of uneasiness; a sense of foreboding.

Breakfast was concluded by seven-thirty. Holmes settled our new acquaintance upon the sofa just as the wind got up and the first branch of lightning lit up the room. I started to count the seconds away...'One Mississippi....Two Mississippi...'

'It is easy to see that your experience has been no common one, Mr. Hatherley,' said he.

'Three Mississippi...'

'Pray, lie down there and make yourself absolutely at home. Tell us what you can, but stop when you are tired, and keep your strength with a little stimulant.'

He placed a pillow beneath his head – Florence Nightingale could not have been sweeter – but then we all jumped out of our skins to a brrrooom! of thunder.

'Four Mississippi! The storm is only four miles away. Steady there, nurse...'

Holmes threw me a jagged glance. 'Oh, ha, ha, ha,' said he, laconically, as he laid a glass of brandy and water within Mr. Hatherley's reach. 'Counting a second in exchange for each mile distant, Doctor, is for infants.'

'But it works, Holmes,' said I, starving him of more criticism, for I knew that I was right.

'Thank you, Mister Holmes,' said my patient, still lisping like a narrow-mouthed serpent, 'but I have felt another man since the doctor bandaged me, and I think that your breakfast has completed the cure.'

'You did very well with your breakfast,' said I. 'It is not very easy to feed oneself when you have a mouth injury, Mr. Hatherley, and only one hand is functioning.'

Indeed. The egg, tomato, steak juice, butter, coffee, strawberry jam, bacon, fish paste, kidney grease, black pudding, claret, marmalade, kipper, orange juice, lobster thermidor and Worcestershire sauce would come out of his shirt-front in the wash. In fact, I noticed that they all caught the light differently in the darkness of the storm and the multiple flashes of electricity forking across the sky. It was a kaleidoscope of colours.

'I shall take up as little of your valuable time as possible, so I shall start at once upon my litany of peculiar experiences that make up my bizarre story.'

Holmes sat in a big armchair, with the weary, heavy-lidded expression which veiled his keen and eager nature, while I sat opposite to him, and we listened in silence to the strange saga which our visitor detailed to us. Brrrooom! Three miles...

'We are all ears, Mister Hatherley,' rasped Holmes, in a deeply baseous voice. 'We shall not interrupt you, will you, Doctor?'

The way Holmes delivered that statement in a gloomy room that was so dark now it was like dusk, with a haggard man peering haunted eyes at me, gave me prickles. I had the feeling that I was settling in to hear Mary Shelley tell me a bedtime story, and I was not far wrong.

'You must know,' said Mr. Hatherley, 'that I am an orphan and a bachelor, residing alone in lodgings in London.

A bachelor? He would be buying a new shirt...

'By profession I am a hydraulic engineer. I have had considerable experience of my work during the seven years that I was apprenticed to Venner & Matheson, the well-known firm of Greenwich. Two years ago, having served my time, and having also come into a fair sum of money through my poor father's death, I determined to start in business for myself, and took professional chambers in Victoria Street.

Mr. Hatherley had dribbled more of his breakfast down his shirt than into his stomach.

'I suppose that everyone finds his first independent start in business a dreary experience. To me it has been exceptionally so. During these past two years I have had only three consultations and one small job, and that is absolutely all that my profession has brought me. My gross takings amount to twenty-seven pounds ten. Every day, from nine in the morning until four in the afternoon, I waited in my little den, until at last my heart began to sink, and I came to believe that I should never have any practice at all'

Holmes interrupted Mr. Hatherley by clearing his throat, suddenly, just as a huge bolt of lightning lit up the sky three or four times over.

'Please do not concern yourself. We are familiar with your predicament: to set up in practice and to have no clients, are you not, Doctor?' Holmes raised his eyebrows above a silly, provocative smile.

I blanched and jumped up, in time with the multiple thunder crashes (two miles). 'Holmes, please! Don't put the needle in about the failure of my medical practice!'

'My apologies, Mr. Hatherley. It is a silly *jeu d'esprit* between us,' said the great detective. 'Pray, continue.'

'Yesterday, just as I was thinking of leaving the office, my clerk entered to say there was a gentleman waiting who wished to see me upon business. He brought up a card, too, with the name Colonel Lysander Stark" engraved upon it."

There seemed to be a surfeit of colonels this week...

'Close at heels came the Colonel himself, a man rather over the middle size but he was a fattish chap with a pinched face. His whole face sharpened away into a nose and chin, and the skin of his cheeks was drawn quite tense over his outstanding bones. Yet this emaciation seemed to be in his natural habit, and due to no disease, for his eye was bright, his step brisk, and his bearing assured. He was plainly but neatly dressed, and his age, I should judge, would be nearer forty than thirty.

'"Mr. Hatherley?"' said he, with something of a German accent. "You haff been recommended to me, Herr. Hatherley, as be-ink a man who iss not only proficient in his profession but iss also discreet and capable of keep-ink a secret."

'Bowed, feeling as flattered as any young man would at such an address. "May I ask who it is who gave me such a good character?" I asked.

'"Well, perhaps it is better that I should not tell you just at zis moment. I haff it from ze same source that you are both an orphan *und* a bachelor and are resid-ink alone in London, am I not correct"'

'"That is quite correct," I answered, "but you will excuse me when I say that I cannot see how all this bears upon my professional qualifications. I understood that it was upon a professional matter that you wished to speak to me?'

'"Undoubtedly zo! But you will find that all I say is to the point. I haff a professional commission for you, but ze absolute secrecy is essential! Absolute secrecy! You understand? And, off course, we expect that more from a man who iss alone than from one who lives in the breast of his family."

'"Bosom,' said I, and the Colonel nodded his acceptance. 'If I promise to keep a secret, you may absolutely depend upon my doing so."

'He looked so very hard at me as I spoke, and it seemed to me that I have never seen so suspicious and questioning eye.'

'"Zo, you do promise me, then?" said he at last.

'"Yes, I promise."

'"Absolute and complete silence, before, during, and after? No reference to the matter at all, either in word or writing?"

'"I have already given you my word."

"Very good." He suddenly sprang up, and darting like lightning across the room, he flung open the door. The passage outside was empty.

'"That iss good," said he, coming back. "I know that clerks are sometimes curious as to their master's affairs. Now we can talk in safety." He drew up his chair very close to mine and began to stare at me again with the same questioning and thoughtful look.

Suddenly some bolts of lightning lit up the room. A second later the whole house was shaken to its foundations, the china chinking, the furniture trembling and my nerves tingling. The storm was sitting almost over us!

'A feeling of repulsion and of something akin to fear had begun to rise within me at the strange antics of this fleshless man. Even my dread of losing a client could not restrain me from showing my impatience.

'"I beg that you will state your business, sir" said I; 'my time is of value."

'Heaven forgive me for that last sentence, but the words came to my lips.'

'"How would fifty guineas for one night's work suit you?" he asked.

'"Most admirably."

'"I say a night's work, but one hour will be sufficient. Simply, I demand your opinion about a stamping machine which has hass gone out off gear. If you show us what iss wrong we shall set it right ourselves. What do you think of such a commission ass good ass that?"

'"The work appears to be light and the pay munificent."

BRRROOOM! We were shaken in our seats by the latest thunderclap.

'"Precisely zo. You will come tonight by the last train."

'"Where to?"

'"To Sunningdale. It is in Berkshire. It is a small place near Ascot, and within seven miles off nowhere. There is a railway locomotive from Waterloo which would bring you there at precisely eleven-fifteen."

'"Very good."

'"I shall be coming down in a carriage to meet you."

'"There is a drive, then?"

'"Yess! Our... my place is out in the country. It is seven miles, remember!!"

'"Yes my apologies. Then we can hardly get there before midnight. I suppose there would be no chance of a train back. I should be compelled to stop the night."

'"Yess! We will give you a shakedown."

'"That is very awkward. Could I not come at some more convenient hour?"

'"*Nein!* We have judged it! You will come late! It is to recompense you for any inconvenience that we are paying you. You, a young man, for which a fee of zis size would buy us an opinion from the very heads off your profession. Still, off course, if you would like to withdraw from zis business, you may do it now..."

'I thought of the fifty guineas, and of how very useful they would be to me.'

BRRROOOMM!

'"No, no, not at all," said I: "I shall be very happy to accommodate myself to your wishes. I should like, however, to understand a little more clearly what it is that you wish me to do."

'"*Gut! Zo istis, ja!* It iss only natural that the pledge of secrecy which we haff exacted from you should have aroused your curiosity. I haff no wish to commit you to anything without having it all laid before you. I suppose that we are absolutely safe from eavesdroppers?"

'"Entirely."

'"Then this matter stands thus... You are probably aware that the fuller's earth iss a valuable product, and that it iss only found in one or two places in England?"

'"I have heard so."

'"Some time ago I infested in a small property – a very small place – within ten miles off Ascot. I was fortunate enough to discover that there was a deposit of fuller's earth in one off my fields. Upon examination, I found that this deposit was a comparatiffly small one, *und* it formed a link between two ferry much larger ones. One upon the right. The uzzer upon the left. Both of them in the grounds off my neighbours! These good people were *dumbkofs!* Ignorant that their land contained that which was as valuable as a gold mine! Naturally, it wass to my advantage to buy the land before they discovered its true value; but, unfortunately, I had no capital by which to do this. But, Herr Hatherley, I took a few of my friends into the secret and they suggested that we should quietly and secretly work our own little deposit. In this way we should earn the money! We would then buy the fields of my neighbours. Thiss... we have now been doing for some time, and in order to help us in our operations we erected a press off the hydraulic kind. This press, as I have explained already is now out of order. We wish your advice upon the subject. But, be warned! We guard our secret ferry jealously! Iff it once became known that we had engineers coming to our *haus*, it would soon cause inquiry. Then, iff the facts were exposed it would be *auf wiedersehen* to stealing the fields and executing our plans. That is why I haff made you promise me that you will not tell any human being living that you are going to Sunningdale tonight. I haff made it all plain, *hein*?"

'"I quite follow you," said I. "The only point which I could not quite understand was what use you could make of a hydraulic press in excavating fuller's earth, which, as I understand, is dug out like gravel from a pit."

'"Ah!" said he carelessly, "we have our own process. We compress the earth into bricks, so as to remove them without revealing what they are. But that is mere detail. I have taken you fully into my confidence now, Mr. Hatherley, and I have shown you how I trust you." He rose as he spoke. "I shall expect you, then, at Sunningdale, at 11.15."

'"I shall certainly be there."

'"Do not speak a word to anyone!" He looked at me with a last, long, questioning gaze, and then, pressing my hand in a cold, dank grasp, he hurried from the room.'

KER-BLANG! All the lights went out. Soot cascaded down the chimney and onto the hearth rug. We heard a scream emanating from somewhere in the house.

Holmes clapped his and together and gave a grinning smile of appreciation. 'Bravo, Mister Hatherley! Or should I address you as Herr Hatherley? Your German accent iss remarkably Prussian *und* excellent!'

'Well, thank you, Mister Holmes!'

'*Herr Holmes*!' quipped I. '*Was ist ihre meinung zu diesem geheimnis*?'

'Watson?' said Holmes, his eyes popping at my linguistic talent. '*Lassen zie den Mann zuerst seine geschichte beeenden*! *Und dein deutsch ist scheibe...*'

'*Mein deutsch ist besser als deins, du pennerloch...*'

Holmes was astounded! So I pre-empted him: 'My first batman was German, Holmes. The one I had in Afghanistan. He called it the only true language of love.'

'Well, he was wrong there, Watson. French or Italian maybe, but German is the language of lust. And fetish? Yes, the language of lust and fet...

KER-BLANG!

'Phew! That was the loudest yet!' remarked our storyteller. 'Now, let me tell you, gentlemen, I was very much astonished, as you may think, at this sudden commission which had been entrusted to me. On the one hand, of course, I was glad, for the fee was at least tenfold what I should have asked had I set a price upon my services, and it was possible that this order might lead to other ones. On the other hand, the face and manner of my patron had made an unpleasant impression upon me, and I could not think that his explanation of fuller's earth was sufficient to explain the necessity for my coming at midnight, and his extreme anxiety lest I should tell anyone of my errand. However, I threw all my fears to the winds, ate a hearty supper, drove to Waterloo, and started off, having obeyed to the letter the injunction as to holding my tongue.

'I arrived at the dimly-lit Sunningdale railway station at eleven o'clock. I was the only passenger who got out there, and there was no one on the platform save a single sleepy porter with a lantern. As I passed out through the wicket-gate, however, I found my acquaintance of the morning waiting in the shadow upon the other side. Without a word he grasped my arm and hurried me into a carriage, the door of which was standing open. He drew up the windows on either side, tapped the woodwork, and away we went as hard as the horse would go.'

'One horse?' interjected Holmes.

'Yes, only one.'

'And was its name Dinsmore Nuisance?' I mentioned blandly, as if in passing.

'Shut up, Watson!'

"I beg your pardon, Doctor?'

'Mister Hatherley, ignore him. Did you happen to observe the colour of the horse?'

'Yes, I saw it by the sidelights when I was stepping into the carriage. It was a chestnut.'

'Tired-looking or fresh?'

'Me? Or the horse?'

'The horse.'

‘Oh, he was fresh and glossy.’

‘Thank you. I am sorry – now it is me who has interrupted you. Pray continue your most interesting statement.’

‘Well, Mister Holmes, away we went! And we drove for at least an hour. Colonel Lysander Stark had said that it was only seven miles, but I should think, from the rate that we seemed to go, and the time that we took, that it must have been nearer twelve. He sat at my side in silence all the time, and I was aware, more than once when I glanced in his direction, that he was looking at me with great intensity. The country roads seemed to be not very good in that part of the world, for we lurched and jolted terribly. I tried to look out of the windows to see something of where we were, but they were made of frosted glass, and I could see nothing save an occasional blur of a passing light. Now and then I hazarded some remark to break the monotony of the journey, but the Colonel answered only in monosyllables, and the conversation soon flagged.’

I started at this. I wanted to say: “what a devil of a foreigner!” but Holmes was giving me a mighty hawkish stare, his head resting on long, white steepled fingers. It was one of his looks that delivered the message: Beware! So, I held my tongue.

‘At last, however, the bumping of the road was exchanged for the crisp smoothness of a gravel drive and the carriage came to a stand. Colonel Lysander Stark sprang out, and, as I followed after him, pulled me swiftly into a porch which gaped in front of us. The instant that I had crossed the threshold the door slammed heavily behind us, and I heard faintly the rattle of the wheels as the carriage drove away.

'It was pitch dark inside the house, and the Colonel fumbled about looking for matches, and muttering under his breath. Suddenly a door opened at the other end of the passage, and a long, golden bar of light shot out in our direction. It grew broader, and a woman appeared with a lamp in her hand, which she held above her head, pushing her face forwards and peering at us. I could see that she was pretty, and from the gloss with which the light shone upon her dark dress I knew that it was a rich material. She spoke a few words in a foreign tongue in a tone as though asking a question, and when my companion answered in a gruff monosyllable she gave such a start that the lamp nearly fell from her hand. Colonel Stark whispered something in her ear, and then, pushing her back into the room from whence she had come, he walked toward me again with the lamp in his hand.'

'"Perhaps you will have the kindness to wait in this room for a few minutes." said he, throwing open another door. It was a quiet little room, plainly furnished with a round table in the centre, on which several German books were scattered. Colonel Stark set down the lamp on the top of a harmonium beside the door. "I shall not keep you waiting an instant," said he, and vanished into the darkness.'

Holmes was completely captivated by the engineer's story and now, cleverly, Mr. Hatherley leaned forward towards us, lowered his voice to his whisper and drew us further into his horror story.

'Gentlemen, this was a *woefully* silent house! There was only an old clock ticking loudly somewhere in the passage, but otherwise everything was deadly still.' He paused, and swivelled his head side-to-side, ever so slowly... Then, suddenly, he went into a fit of wobbling and emitted an horrendous baying sound through his lips: 'BRRRRRR!!!'

Holmes and I jumped up out of our seats! When we landed we exchanged glances of nervous intolerance before flicking our eyes back over to our storyteller.

'I walked across to the window, hoping that I might catch some glimpse of the countryside, but an oak shutter, heavily barred, was folded across it. A vague feeling of uneasiness began to steal over me. Who were these German people, and what were they doing, living in this strange, out-of-the-way place? And where was the place? I was ten miles or so from Sunningdale, that was all I knew, but whether north, south, east, or west, I had no idea. For that matter, Ascot, and possibly any other large town, like Reading or Slough, were within that radius, so the place might not be so secluded after all. Yet it was quite certain from the absolute stillness that we were in the country. I paced up and down the room humming a tune under my breath to keep up my spirits and feeling that I was thoroughly earning my fifty guineas fee.'

Mr. Hatherley paused, drew a huge long breath and rolled his eyes, ready to deliver the next, devastating instalment of his daunting story. He lowered his head into his chest. We moved in even closer so as not to miss the merest syllable in the ghostly silence. You could hear a pin drop!

'SUDDENLY!' he barked, and both of our *derrières* launched up once again from our chairs; 'without any warning,' he whispered, 'and without any preliminary sound in the midst of the utter stillness... the door... of my room... swung.... slowwwwly...'

My hair stood up! My breath held short! My perineum pulsated!

'OPEN!' The door swung open and there, standing in the aperture, was the woman! The darkness of the hall was behind her! And the yellow light of my lamp was beating upon her eager and beautiful face! But, gentlemen, that beautiful countenance was... SICK WITH FEAR! So sick that the sight sent a chill to my own heart!'

Blimey! This Mr. Hatherley knew how to tell a ghost story!

'She held up one shaking finger. It was to warn me to be silent. She shot a few whispered words of broken English at me, her eyes glancing back, like those of a frightened horse, into the gloom behind her.

'"I would go," said she, trying hard, as it seemed to me, to speak calmly; "I should not stay here. There is no good for you to do. Go, now!"

'"But madam," said I, "I have not yet done what I came for. I cannot possibly leave until I have seen the machine."

'"It is not worth your while to wait," she went on. "You can pass through the door; no one hinders." And then, seeing that I smiled and shook my head, she whispered: "Get away from here before it is too late!"

'But I am somewhat headstrong by nature, and the more ready to engage in an affair when there is some obstacle in the way. I thought of my fifty-guinea fee, of my wearisome journey, and of the unpleasant night which seemed to be before me. Was it all to go for nothing? Why should I slink away without having carried out my commission, and without the payment which was my due? This woman might, for all I knew, be a monomaniac. With a stout bearing, therefore, though her manner had shaken me more than I cared to confess, I still shook my head, and declared my intention to remain where I was. She was about to renew her entreaties when a door slammed overhead, and the sound of several footsteps were heard upon the stairs. She listened for an instant, threw up her hands with a despairing gesture, and vanished as noiselessly as she had come.

'The new-comers were Colonel Lysander Stark, and a short thick man with a chinchilla beard growing out of the creases of his double chin, who was introduced to me as Mr. Ferguson.

'"This Ferguson is my secretary and manager," said the Colonel. "By the way, I was under the impression that I had left this door shut just now. I fear that you have felt the draught."

'"On the contrary," said I, "I opened the door myself, because I felt the room to be a little close."

'He shot one of his suspicious glances at me. "Perhaps we had better proceed to business then," said he. "Mister Ferguson and I will take you up to see the machine."

'"I had better put my hat on, I suppose."

'"Oh no, it is in the house."

'"What, do you dig fuller's earth in the house?"

'"No, no. This is only where we compress it. But never mind that! All we wish you to do is to examine the machine and to let us know what is wrong with it."

We went upstairs together, the Colonel first with the lamp, the fat manager and I behind him. It was a labyrinth of an old house, with corridors, passages, narrow winding staircases, and little low doors, the thresholds of which were hollowed out by the generations who had crossed them. There were no carpets, and no signs of any furniture above the ground floor, while the plaster was peeling off the walls, and the damp was breaking through in green, unhealthy blotches. I tried to put on as unconcerned an air as possible, but I had not forgotten the warnings of the lady, even though I disregarded them, and I kept a keen eye upon my two companions. Ferguson appeared to be a morose and silent man, but I could see from the little he said that he was at least a fellow countryman.

'Colonel Lysander Stark stopped at last before a low door, which he unlocked. Within was a small square room, in which the three of us could hardly fit into at one time. Ferguson remained outside, and the Colonel ushered me in.

'"We are now,' said he, "actually within the hydraulic press, and it would be a particularly unpleasant thing for us if anyone were to turn it on. The ceiling of this small chamber is really the end of a descending piston, and it comes down with the force of many tons upon this metal floor. There are small lateral columns of water outside which receive the force, and which transmit and multiply it in the manner which is familiar to you. The machine goes readily enough, but there is some stiffness in the working of it and it has lost a little of its force. Perhaps you will have the goodness to look it over, and to show us how we can set it right."

'I took the lamp from him, and I examined the machine very thoroughly. It was indeed a gigantic one, and capable of exercising enormous pressure. When I passed outside, however, and pressed down the levers which controlled it, I knew at once by the whishing sounds that there was a slight leakage, which allowed a regurgitation of water through one of the side-cylinders. An examination showed that one of the india-rubber bands which was round the head of a driving-rod had shrunk so as not to quite fill the socket along which it worked. This was clearly the cause of the loss of power.'

What language! Well, gentlemen readers, if your driving-rod didn't fill the rubber it was a dead certainty to cause a nasty leak, wouldn't you say?! It was only when Mr. Hatherley and Sherlock Holmes were staring at me agog that I realised that I had just said that out loud. Oops...

'My apologies, gentlemen. Sometimes, one's motor neurone overtakes the rest of one's brain...'

'Please!' said he, holding up his hand, his good hand, 'do not apologise, Doctor. My goodness, we could use some levity in this situation.' Hatherley paused. He became thoughtful, raising his eyes to the heavens, before levelling his eyes onto mine. 'Because it is about to get much, much worse!'

I gulped. I nodded, guiltily.

'Yes, do shut up, Watson! Pray, continue with you story of abject horror, Mister Hatherley...'

'Yes, I pointed out where the machine's problem lay with my two companions, who followed my remarks very carefully, and asked several practical questions as to how they should proceed to set it right. When I had made it clear to them, I returned to the main chamber of the machine, and took a good look at it to satisfy my own curiosity. It was obvious at a glance that the story of the fuller's earth was the merest fabrication, for it would be absurd to suppose that so powerful an engine could be designed for so inadequate a purpose. The walls were of wood, but the floor consisted of a large iron trough, and when I came to examine it I could see a crust of metallic deposit all over it. I had stooped and was scraping at this to see exactly what it was, when I heard a muttered exclamation in German, and saw the cadaverous face of the Colonel looking down at me.

'"What are you doing there?" he asked.

'I felt angry at having been tricked by so an elaborate story as that which he had told me. "I was admiring your fuller's earth," said I: "I think that I should better able to advise you as to your machine if I knew what the exact purpose was for which it was used."

'The instant that I uttered the words I regretted the rashness of my speech. His face set hard, and a baleful light sprang up in his eyes.

'"Very well," said he, "you shall know all about the machine." He took a step backward, slammed the little door, and turned the key in the lock. I rushed towards it and pulled the handle, but it was quite secure, and did not give in the least to my kicks and shoves. "Hello!" I yelled. "Hello! Colonel! Let me out!"

Our storyteller jumped up out of his chair, now thoroughly worked up and animated, his eyes blazing and arms gesticulating, like a willow tree in a gale-force wind.

'And then suddenly in the silence I heard a sound which sent my heart into my mouth. I heard a noise which sounded very similar to a bicycle being ridden. There was a clank of levers being activated and the swish of the leaking cylinder. He had set the engine at work! The lamp still stood upon the floor where I had placed it when examining the trough. By its light I saw that the black ceiling was coming down upon me; slowly, jerkily, but, as none knew better than myself, with a force which must within a minute grind me to a shapeless pulp. I threw myself, screaming, against the door, and dragged with my nails at the lock! I implored the Colonel to let me out, but the remorseless clanking of the levers drowned my cries. The ceiling was descending upon me! It was not long before it was only a foot or two above my head, and with my hand upraised I could feel the hard, rough surface. Then it flashed through my mind that the pain of my death would depend very much on the position in which I met it. If I lay on my face the weight would come down upon my spine, and I shuddered to think of that dreadful snap. Easier the other way, perhaps, and yet had I the nerve to lie and look up at the deadly black shadow wavering down upon me? Already I was unable to stand erect, when my eyes caught something which brought a gush of hope back to my heart.

'I have said that though the floor and ceiling were made of iron, the walls were of wood. As I gave a last hurried glance around, I saw a thin line of yellow light between two of the boards, which broadened and broadened as a small panel was loose and pushed backwards. For an instant I could hardly believe that there was a door which would make sure that I escaped death, but there it was! I threw myself through head-first, as if I was diving into a pond. The panel had closed again behind me, but the crash of the lamp, and a few moments afterwards the clang of the two slabs of metal, told me how narrow had been my escape.'

Holmes and I both heaved a huge sigh of relief. Mr. Hatherley sat himself back down in his chair. He still had an uncomfortable look about him and was very nervous.

'There is more, gentlemen, much more,' said he, nervously twiddling his fingers and his one remaining thumb. 'I was dazed by the dive and the landing after upon the stone floor of a corridor,' he continued, 'but I was recalled to myself by a frantic plucking at my wrist. The same woman whose warning I had rejected was bent over me, tugging me with her left hand, while she held a candle in her right.

'"Come! Come!" she cried breathlessly. "They will be here in a moment! They will see that you are not in there. Oh, do not waste the precious time, but come with me now!"

'This time at least I did not scorn her advice. I staggered to my feet and ran with her along the corridor and down a winding stair. The latter led to another broad passage, and, just as we reached it we heard the sound of running feet and the shouting of two voices – one was answering the other – from the floor on which we were, and from one beneath. My guide stopped and looked about her, like one who is at her wits' end. Then she threw open a door which led into a bedroom, through the window of which the moon was shining brightly.

'"It is your only chance," said she. "It is high up, but you will have to jump it."

'Jump?! From the second floor? She had to be kidding! But as she spoke a light sprang into view at the further end of the passage, and I saw the lean figure of Colonel Stark running forward with a lantern in one hand, and a weapon like a butcher's cleaver in the other. I rushed across the bedroom, flung open the window, and looked out. How quiet and sweet and wholesome the garden looked in the moonlight, and it could not be more than thirty feet down. I clambered out upon the sill, but I hesitated to jump. She shouted to the Colonel: "I will stop him from talking!" She rushed up to me, clasped my face in her hands and kissed me, and when I say "kissed" I mean a deep, passionate kiss, like I had never experienced before!'

What a story! Holmes and I raised our eyebrows in unison and made gasps of "typical continental!" and "whatever next?' and "did you get her name and address?"

'But then I felt this incredible pain shooting through my tongue. I shouted out loud, but my voice was stifled by my own blood! She ran off to return to the door and held it closed, to give me a chance to jump and escape. I heard my lusty saviour arguing with the baby-faced ruffian who pursued me. Then he was pushing the door open, crashing his way past her. But she threw her arms around him and tried to hold him back.

'"Lysander, *mein brüder*!" she cried, "remember your promise after the last man? You promised you would not kill again!" She pointed to me. "*Er wird schweigen!* Oh, he will be silent! Look! Here I have his tongue!"

'She pushed two of her fingers into her mouth and pulled out some messy pink blob. Oh my God, Mister Holmes, she had bitten off my tongue!'

Holmes and I jumped up out of our seats. 'So, that explains the lisp?' I cried.

'Yes, Doctor. Sadly, she is the cause of my speech impediment.'

'Don't stop there, Mister Hatherley!' ordered Sherlock Holmes. 'Continue!'

Holmes and I fell back into our chairs.

'Well, Mister Holmes, Doctor... The woman pushed my tongue back into her mouth and masticated like mad dog. Then... she swallowed it!'

Holmes and I had never experienced a sushi cannibal before. There are no words to suitably describe the horror that we felt. Mr. Hatherley gauged our reaction and continued with his story.

'The Colonel shouted at her: "You are a mad kisser Elise, but you will ruin us! This man hass seen too much. Let me pass! Get out off my way!" He dashed her to one side, and, rushed towards me. I climbed out of the window as fast as I could and just as I was hanging with my fingers on the sill he cut at me with his heavy weapon. When his blow fell I was conscious of a dull pain in my hand. My grip loosened and I fell into the garden below.

'I was shaken, but not hurt by the fall, so I picked myself up and rushed off among the bushes as hard as I could run, for I understood that I was far from being out of danger yet. I glanced down at my hand, which was throbbing painfully, and then, for the first time, saw that my thumb had been cut off, and that the blood was pouring from my wound. I endeavoured to tie my handkerchief round it, but there came a sudden buzzing in my ears, and the next moment I fell dead faint among the rose bushes.'

'How long I remained unconscious I cannot tell. It must have been a very long time, for the moon had sunk and a bright morning was breaking when I came to myself. My clothes were all sodden with dew, and my coat-sleeve was drenched with blood from my wounded thumb. The smarting of it recalled in an instant all the particulars of my night's adventure, and I sprang to my feet with the feeling that I might hardly yet be safe from my pursuers. But, to my astonishment, when I came to look around me neither house nor garden were to be seen. I had been lying in an angle of the hedge close by the highroad, and just a little lower down was a long building, which proved, upon my approaching it, to be the very station at which I had arrived upon the previous night. Were it not for the ugly wound upon my hand, and the fact that I was missing the tip of my tongue, all that had passed during those dreadful hours might have been an evil dream?

'Half dazed, I went into the station. The same porter was on duty, I found, as had been there when I arrived. I inquired from him whether he had ever heard of Colonel Lysander Stark. The name was strange to him. Had he observed a carriage the night before waiting for me? No, he had not. Was there a police station anywhere near? There was one, about three miles off.

'I set off on the road in search of it, observing the directions given to me. But it was too far for me to go, weak and ill as I was. After about a mile, I took refuge in the nearest house I stumbled upon. It happened to be the house taken by Prince Soltykoff during Ascot week. I used up my last energy to rap upon the front door and fainted once again.

'Speaking as a physician who has operated as an army medic on the front line of war, I say that you are most fortunate,' said I, 'to have lost so much blood and be sitting here telling us your story.'

Mr. Hatherley's first flying lesson!

'You must have seen some terrible wounds, Doctor Watson?'

'I thought that I had seen everything... until I met Mister Sherlock Holmes. Squashing people, chopping off their thumbs and biting out their tongues is a new frontier for me Mister Hatherley! You must have a constitution of iron.'

We both sat in silence for some little time after listening to this extraordinary narrative. Then Sherlock Holmes stood up from his chair and walked around the room with his head bowed and his hand cupping his chin. He tapped his finger against his lips. I could tell that the master detective was in deep pontification. Suddenly, he lifted his finger in triumph and stopped his ambulation.

'I have something that will interest you!' said he. 'There was an advertisement which appeared in all the papers about a year ago. It concerned the whereabouts of Mr. Jeremiah Hayling, aged 26, who had gone missing. He was an hydraulic engineer. He left his lodgings at ten o'clock at night. And has not been heard of since. Ha! That represents the last time that the Colonel needed to have his machine overhauled, I fancy.'

'Good heavens!,' cried my patient. 'Then that explains what the girl said.'

'Undoubtedly! It is quite clear that the Colonel was a cool and desperate man, who was absolutely determined that nothing should stand in the way of his little game, like those out-and-out pirates who will leave no survivor from a captured ship. Well, every moment now is precious, so if you feel equal to it, we shall send two telegrams at once as a preliminary to starting off for Sunningdale railway station: one marked "very urgent" to Scotland Yard and the other tagged "extremely urgent" to the Oxford University Museum of Natural History.'

* * *

Some two hours later we were all at the railway station together. There was Sherlock Holmes and I, both of us dressed in our best morning coats and silkiest toppers ready to go racing. Also, Mr. Hatherley, the one-thumbed hydraulic engineer with-a-lisp, Inspector Bradstreet* of Scotland Yard, and a plain-clothes man who bore the look of a typical Londoner. A telegram had arrived for Holmes, which he was so pleased to receive he emitted an ejaculation on the spot! Elated, he glanced over it without comment and tucked it away into his coat pocket.

Bradstreet had spread an ordnance map of the neighbouring country upon the station master's desk, rather carelessly as it turned out as he was now extinguishing the flames after placing it over the station master's pipe tray. Once he had that under control he spread it out again and set to with his compass, drawing a circle with Sunningdale as its centre.

'There you are,' said he. 'That circle is drawn at the radius of ten miles from the village here. the place we want must be somewhere near that line. You said ten miles, I think, sir?'

'It was an hour's good drive.'

'And you think that they brought you back all that way when you were unconscious?'

'They must have done so. I have a confused memory, too, of having been lifted and conveyed somewhere.'

* see *The Man with the Hairy Face*

'What I cannot understand,' said I, 'is why they should have spared you when they found you lying fainting in the garden. This theorem is bollocks!'

'I agree with your Anglo-Saxon view on life, Doctor. I never saw a more inexorable face in my life in Colonel Stark.'

'Oh, we shall soon clear up all that,' said Bradstreet. 'Well, I have drawn my circle, and I only wish I knew at what point upon it the folk that we are in search of are to be found.'

'I think I could lay my finger on it,' said Holmes quietly.

'Really. Now!' cried the inspector, 'you have formed your opinion! Come now, we shall see who agrees with you. I say it is south, for the country is more deserted there.'

'And I say east' said my patient.

'I am for west,' remarked the plain-clothes man. 'There are several quiet little villages up there.'

'And I am for north,' said I, 'because there are no hills there, and our friend says that he did not notice the carriage go up any.'

'Come,' said the inspector, laughing. 'It is a very pretty diversity of opinion. We have boxed the compass among us. Who do you give your casting vote to, Mister Holmes?'

'You are all wrong.'

'But we can't *all* be.'

'Oh, yes you can. This is my point,' he placed his finger on the centre of the circle. 'This is where we shall find them.'

'But the twelve-mile drive?' gasped Hatherley.

'Six and six back. Nothing simpler. You say yourself that the horse was fresh and glossy when you got in. How could it be that, if it had gone twelve miles over heavy roads?'

'Indeed it is a likely ruse enough,' observed Bradstreet thoughtfully. 'Of course there can be no doubt as to the nature of this gang.'

'None at all,' said Holmes. 'They are coiners on a large scale and have used the machine to form an amalgam which has taken the place of silver.'

'We have known for some time that a clever gang was at work,' said the inspector. 'They have been turning out half-crowns by the thousand. We even traced them as far as Reading but could get no further, for they had covered their traces in a way that showed that they were very old hands. But now, thanks to this lucky chance, I think that we have got them right enough.'

'Only once you know precisely where they are, Inspector,' remarked Holmes, rolling his eyes at the blundering ineptitude of the police force.'

'Well, you have a good point there, Mister Holmes!' blustered the inspector.

'And for that, you need me,' said Sherlock Holmes, with a sly grin on his face. 'Come!'

We rolled out of Sunningdale railway station and followed Sherlock Holmes. He marched down the road at a brisk pace, confident in his stride, head held high, swinging his cane forward and smacking its metal tip firmly onto the tarmac with each step, and we all followed like sheep. We walked for about ten minutes. I drew alongside my esteemed companion to warn him that we had limited time for meandering about Berkshire before we were due back at Ascot racecourse for day three of the meeting. Now, what you are unaware of dear adventure-enthusiast, is that thanks to Holmes's skill at the bridge table the previous evening, we had a ton of money, enough to restore the gambling fund with which to back the Jewish horse, Gold, to win the Gold Cup. Holmes acknowledged me with a mischievous smile and said: *'du spricht Deutsch, was?'* and increased his pace. Then, the two policemen started to whine and bleat about the lack of information and ribbed Holmes to obfuscation about his orienteering. Then, just before the road topped a low hill, there was a great widespread whitewashed building in front of us. Holmes stopped us and extended his arm out by way of a graceful flourish of his cane to make an introduction to the house.

'That's it!' cried Hatherley, in intense excitement. 'There is the gravel drive, and there are the rose bushes where I lay. That second window is the one that I jumped from.'

'Good!' said Holmes chuckling away at his cleverness, and much to the delicious chagrin of the Scotland Yard coppers, who looked like they had been sucking on lemons. 'Now, inspector, how would you like to trap your birds?'

Bradstreet and his plain-clothes man surveyed the building and conferred for what seemed like an hour but was, in fact, about a minute.

'I shall go through the front door, Mister Holmes, and my colleague, Jolyon, here will go around to the rear, just in case they make a run for it.'

Jolyon! Really? We sniggered.

'Masterful, Inspector! What could go wrong with that uneven match of three versus two?'

'Well, I shall tell you why, Mister Holmes. One of the three adversaries is a woman, hardly a match for the strapping young *Jolyon* here and my good self, would you not say?'

'But Inspector, this woman you speak of is no shy spinster. She bites the tongues out of grown men's mouths!'

Inspector Bradstreet took a step backwards, his cow-horn moustache bristling with shock.

'And then... she masticates!' said I, rubbing in the gruesomeness by pretending to chew an imaginary steak. 'Like a mad-possessed cannibal!' I mock-swallowed, for full effect.

'Oh, my God, no!' cried the Inspector. 'We don't stand a chance!'

'Gawd blimey, Doc!' opined Jolyon, in a funny, high-pitched voice. 'What an 'orrible creature she must be! Good job I got this...' And he produced a 0.38 revolver from his shoulder-holster.

Holmes raised his eyebrows on sight of the gun. 'But may I suggest, Inspector, that we may gain the upper hand on these villains if Watson and I were to sneak in via the rear of the domicile and flush these fine birds out via the front door and straight into the arms of the law?'

'That is the sort of idea that we like to hear, Mister Holmes,' said Bradstreet, whilst Jolyon nodded and Bradstreet withdrew his revolver from his armpit.

'Ah! You are armed.'

'Oh, yes. We each own a revolver.'

"We are not protected. We shall take one of yours and you keep the other?'

'No, Mister Holmes, that would mean that we have only one.'

'But then it follows that you will have two and the Doctor and I will have none.'

'Quite so, Mister Holmes. Now, shall we place ourselves into position?'

To say that the great detective looked piqued was an understatement. But, with a twirl of his cane, he made a swift recovery, the scent of his quarry now thick in his nostrils outside the lair.

'Come along, Watson. The game's afoot!'

We could not walk straight down the driveway and sidle around to the rear of the house or we would be noticed and challenged. So, with Mr. Hatherley in tow directly behind me, we circumnavigated the property via a gully which ran down the boundary with its neighbour. After the recent thunderstorm it was a little treacherous, to say the least, and I sank down to my knees on a couple of occasions. The master detective was in an ebullient mood; he seemed to somehow float over the seriously boggy sections chivvying me along – in German, would you believe it – with an occasional "*Achtung, Watson*! *Vorsicht vor dem moor!*" or a "*Beobachten sie, wohen sie gehen, dummkopf*!" but eventually we arrived at the rear of the property and, without any hesitation, slipped inside by the pantry door.

Indoors was dark and foreboding. The pantry led to the kitchen and then onto the rear hallway, which was windowless. We padded our way through the vestibule as quietly as possible but there was a distinct squelching coming from my shoes that spluttered the imposing silence of the sombre house. It was when we rounded the corner into the main hallway itself, which was panelled in oak with a heavily-carved staircase winding up to a half-landing, mid-staircase, from where the whole space was illuminated by a large, stained-glassed window. Unfortunately, standing there on that half landing, mid-staircase, was the imposing figure of a man holding a long, shiny meat chopper in his right hand, hanging low. We stopped dead in our tracks.

'What the devil are you doing here?' cried I. 'Surely you should be with your horses?'

Colonel Blanders threw back his head and emitted a custardy laugh. He was so confident of his superiority that he started a walk down the staircase towards us whilst still laughing so hard that he glissaded the heel of his left shoe on the edge of the first tread, dropped ungainly to the second and only caught his balance on the third riser. That shut him up! He ignored the sarcastic smirk that Holmes and I exchanged.

'No, Doctor Watson,' said he, with restored arrogance, 'my training of thoroughbreds has always been fruitless, but it provides an excellent distraction for the operation that is here.'

'We were expecting to be greeted by a certain Colonel Lysander Stark, of German descent,' remarked Sherlock Holmes. 'What have you done with him?'

'*Aber er ist auch hier, Herr Holmes,*' replied the Colonel. Well, that answered Holmes's question! It turns out that both of the colonels were one and the same.

Holmes's features betrayed an expression of surprise, decanted to mental resolution. 'I suppose I should have known that anyone who trains a horse like Dinsmore Nuisance would need a supplementary income. But I have to confess that I hadn't chanced upon a deduction that would implement you as a counterfeiter, or, indeed, a German.'

'You would not have to strain your brain so hard if you didn't poke your nose into my affairs, *Herr Holmes*!'

'We would not have to be here, Colonel Whateveryournameis,' said I, 'if you didn't chop this person's thumb off!'

'Who?'

I looked round for our client but he was nowhere to be seen!

'Oh! Well, he was right behind me.' My eyes searched the gloom... 'Where *has* he got to?

'He will have been constricted by the bog,' remarked Holmes. "Did you not keep an eye out for him?'

'Another victim, Doctor, of your medical incompetence!' rasped the Colonel.

'What the devil do you refer to, you slanderous square head!'

'I refer to myself! Following your administering of the bowel-loosening drugs into my pink gin, Doctor, I spent all night evacuating into the water closet! And, the day after, I am just as frequent. I even had to make a run of emergency, back to the water closet, whilst I was chasing Mister Hatherley. *Zo*! He escaped, out of the window, I could not make the hunt for him afterwards.

Why? Because I was back in the water closet, that is why! You poisoner, you!'

'Well, Colonel,' said Holmes, 'we have only Doctor Watson to thank for Mister Hatherley's escape. Even so, regardless of your grumbling guts, we have a client who has had his thumb amputated, and I have no doubt that is was the work of that cleaver you are holding there.'

'And he is missing part of his tongue, all thanks to you, you bounder!' cried I.

'I did not cut it off, Doctor Watson. It was my sister, Elise.'

'I kept telling him to leave the house, but he wouldn't listen to me,' emanated a delicate, wavering voice from above. Holmes and I looked up to see a handsome woman leaning against the bannister, looking down upon us from the landing. 'Three times I warned him. Three times he avoided my advice. When my brother lost his patience, just like he did with the last engineer who came here, I had to try to silence him before Lysander did the same. In a moment of rash spontaneity I bit into his tongue, hoping to numb his ability to talk. Believe me, nobody was more surprised when it came off in my mouth!'

Holmes and I glanced at one another and drew air sharply through our teeth in our own moment of spontaneity.

'Yes, gentlemen, ho ho! My sister is a formidable lady; not to be taken to bed without due care and attention,' quipped the Colonel, smirking, as if it had been part of his plan to dispose of Mr. Hatherley.

'Take no notice of my brother! By nature I am a gentle soul. I wished to save the poor man! I imagined that if he could not talk, he would do us no any harm.' She paused. 'Would he?'

'Well, I suppose he could write down his experiences on some paper?' I offered.

'You have raised a very good point there, Watson,' said Holmes.

'I though it was rather obvious, Holmes, but sometimes these things, you know…'

'STOP IT! That is ENOUGH! Enough of this verbal jousting!' cried Colonel Blanders, as he raised his chopper up to level with Holmes's nose. 'Elise! Go to your room and stay there.' He shook the point at my companion. 'Now it is time, Mister Holmes, and you, poisoner!' He waved his chopper at me. 'To inspect our hydraulic press at close quarters. Lead the way up the stairs.'

'Certainly not!' said Holmes, who capered back a step, in a style of prancing that Dandy Sandy would have been proud of. He drew the sword from the sheath of his walking stick and tapped the blade against the Colonel's cleaver. 'On guard!' cried the great detective, as he assumed a textbook, straight out of Angelo's School of Arms. 'I am a master of the épée. *Allez!*'

Well, of course, he would be a "master of the épée," wouldn't he?

'And I am a crack shot, Mister Holmes,' uttered a voice from the shadows. 'Put it down, or I shall be forced to place a bullet between your eyes.'

It was Mr Ferguson, of course, the third man, whom we had forgotten about.

'*Touchez, Monsieur Ferguson*!' remarked Holmes, dropping his blade to the rest.

Sherlock Holmes's tailor hadn't made provision in the trouser department for swordfighting!

'Let us put a stop to all this foreign ribaldry. German here; French there. Whatever next? Now, you will listen to me. We shall walk up the stairs together. Colonel Stark will lead the way. I shall follow up in the rear. One false move, from any of you, and I shall shoot the person dead. And, as I have just told you: I am a crack shot.'

Ferguson wore a strange facial hair arrangement between his two chins and looked like a man who had been born in a double-breasted suit. He appeared to be resolute, trustworthy and boring. Also, a man who wouldn't brag. He flicked the barrel of his pistol towards the staircase. Holmes sheathed his weapon and followed the Colonel's lead. Just like Mr. Hatherley told us about the day before, we made our way along a myriad of landings and corridors, interspersed with the occasional step or staircase. It was a much larger building than it appeared from the outside, that was for sure. Eventually, we trod on bare staircases and floorboards and arrived at an area that was a sort of mezzanine floor. In front of us was the low door our client had described, and another room adjacent that was new to us, which featured many pipes, hoses and levers. In a dingy corner, almost next to the dividing wall, curiously, somebody had parked a socking great bicycle. It was positioned upright, and when I say that it was large, it was due to its two big wheels, not dissimilar to a contraption I had encountered once at speciality knocking-shop off of Cambridge Circus (all it was missing was the tart on top and my imagination soon put her onto the saddle)!

As there was no natural light. Colonel Lysander Stark-Blanders lit an oil lamp that was positioned on the floor adjacent, located the key on the architrave above and unlocked the door.

'Please, after you,' hissed the Colonel, pointing his chopper into the completely dark room. 'And take this...' he handed me the oil lamp hurriedly.

'Ah, yes, the lamp,' said Holmes. 'But surely you have electricity in this part of the house, Colonel?'

'Do not act dumb to me, Mister Holmes! You know that we have electricity.' He pointed at the large bicycle. 'How else could we operate an engine?'

Holmes nodded his acknowledgement that the bicycle was a magneto but I sensed an air of discomfort about the Colonel. He had turned pallid and was sweating along his top lip. Maybe he could be over-powered? I flashed my eyes over to Ferguson – he had stopped a couple of yards away and was still holding the pistol, awaiting any rash move that I might have in mind. Maybe not, then. I glanced back to the Colonel. Now, he was doing the same thing with his eyes as he had on Tuesday evening at Lord Coventry's. I squinted at him, quizzically, but thankfully Holmes noticed the change of ambience and threw in a perfectly-timed spoiler.

'But why would we accept your kind invitation to visit that room when it is, in fact, an hydraulic press? As soon as we are inside, you will close and lock this door. Then, you will start the engine. What do you think, Doctor?'

'Well, now that you ask me, Holmes, I wouldn't if I was you. Or me, for that matter.'

'Go into the room!' cried Colonel Blanders-Stark-whateverhisnamewas. And his eyes turned livid as he swung the chopper back behind his head in readiness to make a sweeping cut at both of us, such was the small confine that we had been corralled into. I realised, all of a sudden, that I would have to come to more amicable terms with this dual Colonel.

'I say, Colonel Blanders, it was rather mean of me to lace your gin with phenol, but do you not think that this retribution you have planned is just a tad over-the-top? And you have no quarrel with my companion here, Mr. Sherlock Holmes, who is the most famous detective in the land. If he is murdered, it will be Scotland Yard and the gallows for you, and Mr. Crackshot. In fact, Inspector Bradstreet is waiting for us outside this house. Right now!'

Little did I know that as I spoke, Bradstreet and Sergeant Jolyon were digging the single-thumbed, clipped-tongued Mr. Hatherley out of the bog before it consumed him.

'Nobody will know where you have disappeared to, Doctor,' remarked the Colonel smartly. 'This engine is so powerful that it will reduce you both to a slender layer of mush, as thin as photographic film. You will be strawberry jam in a dainty sandwich. There will be no clues.' He shuffled from foot-to-foot and suddenly looked desperate. 'NOW GET IN!' His eyes widened and he swung his chopper back further, in readiness to strike.

'Come along, Watson!' exclaimed Holmes, with a jaunty lift of his swordstick. 'Let us not disappoint our German friend here and his crack-shot sidekick. The game's afoot!'

Those simple words told me that the great detective had solved the case; that he was on top of these villains;

and that he had planned our escape from the hydraulic press.

'HURRY UP!' screamed the Colonel.

'Right-o, Holmes!' said I, and followed Sherlock into the room, still carrying the oil lamp. The door was closed behind us quickly. The lock turned heavily.

Immediately, Holmes and I turned around and placed our ears on the door. We heard the Colonel instruct his sister, Elise, to "mount the bicycle," but then a much louder shout of "*scheizen*!" followed by a scuffle, then the clatter of metal being dropped onto wood – the Colonel discarding his cleaver, no doubt – followed by a rapid pattering of feet and an intermittent thumping on hollow timber.

'Ah! That will be the Colonel leaping down the staircase two risers at-a-time,' said I.

'Making yet another dash for the sanctuary of the water closet,' remarked Holmes. Maybe you should cut the dose of phenol to your next victim, Doctor.'

We heard the bicycle being ridden by Elise, which must have provided power for an electric lamp because we could now see a yellow glow between the panels of the wooden walls. But then we heard a sound that made us ditch our light-heartedness: it was the hydraulic press engine starting up! There were some metallic clanks and a hissing sound as air was forced into the machine and pressurising the hydraulics. I glanced at Holmes. He glanced at me. We heard the clank of a lever being pulled amid some rather excited male voices – obviously, the Colonel had returned – and then, to my horror, there was a whirring sound and the ceiling started to move down towards us. Sherlock Holmes widened his eyes in wonder. A smile crept across his face and he chuckled. He was mesmerised by it!

'Holmes, my dear chap, fascinating though this contraption is, what is this plan you have hatched for our deliverance?'

'Which plan are you referring to?'

'Well, just now, when we were standing outside the room, I could tell by your attitude that you have a plan to get us out of here, in the same state as we arrived?'

'No, I do not. But isn't this machine marvellous?' The ceiling was near enough for him to place his hand.

'Holmes, please!'

The ceiling was touching the top of my head.

'We must make our escape!'

'Surely you remember the engineer's account of this morning. Although the floor and ceiling are made of iron, the walls are of wood. If you look over there, you will find the wooden panel in the wall which is loose, where Mister Hatherley must have made his exit. See! The light chinks through.'

Sure enough, right opposite, there were the two panels that Mr. Hatherley had described to us. I was already being forced into a stoop by the rapidly diminishing height of the room, so my high-speed scuttle forward to the wooden wall was made much easier. I pressed my fingers between the panels to prise them apart and convert the wall into a temporary door, but... nothing moved. NOTHING!

'HOLMES!'

I looked up to see the ceiling now only five feet from the floor.

'What is it now, Doctor?' said he, as calm as a Church pastor on a Monday morning. He was on the other side of the room by the door fiddling with the handle and lock mechanism, which stood proud of the door itself.

'The panel does not move. It has been fixed! Somebody must have mended it!'

'There is German efficiency for you.'

'German efficiency?'

'Yes, they are renowned for their well-ordered society and prompt reaction to things that go bump in the night, like that loose panel there.'

It would not budge. I gave up and stood up but the ceiling was lower, down to four feet, so I was badly hunched.

'I say, Holmes, it is getting a trifle cramped in here...' But then I caught sight of Holmes in a moment of triumph, throwing up his arms in jubilation at the successful pick of the door lock. I smiled. No, I grinned from ear to ear. Sherlock Holmes – the master lock-picker strikes again!*

'There you are,' said he, smiling masterfully at me, 'it is easy when you know how. In fact, my dear Watson, it is elementary.'

I crabbed across the room to him, with now only three and a half feet of headroom. He turned the handle and, sure enough, the door opened up. Sherlock Holmes was a clever man, of that there is no doubt, but there was a problem; and it was an insurmountable problem. The door opened inwards – *into* the room

* see *The Speckled Band Speculation*

– not outwards. Now that the ceiling was only three feet off the floor the door had no space into which to open, thus giving us an exit aperture that was about the width of a panda's penis.

'Bugger!' swore Holmes unusually, and he whisked his hand away from the door handle in the nick of time, just as the ceiling's relentless descent scythed the lock mechanism off the door, handle and all, and smashed it to smithereens. The noise was a reminder of how powerful the hydraulic press was. We slumped down onto the floor together, heavy in heart and becoming anxious.

'Now see here, Holmes, the way the door turned out was desperately disappointing, but, as my Afghan CO said to me one day when we were facing hordes of irritable Ghazis pouring off the hills towards us, vowing to take no prisoners, and outnumbering us five to one: "What the fuck are we going to do?"'

'I am glad your commanding officer said that because it is very apt for our predicament and I know that you would not use that type of language.'

'Perish the thought! But I say, Holmes, we are only two and a half feet from meeting our maker, what shall we do?'

He pondered for a moment and then looked me in the eye. 'We have been friends for a while now, Watson.' It was the sort of inquiring eye that demanded satisfaction. 'If we are going to die, perhaps there is something I should know and you have been meaning to tell me?'

Goodness, did he mean my affair with Rachel? Well, when I say affair we had never actually done it, so maybe no. Or was it the five thousand guineas that I took from the King of Bohemia to pay for my marriage annulment to Mary and had yet to tell him?

'Like what, Holmes?'

'Maybe something that you felt was too awkward? Or too embarrassing for you?'

Goodness, was he was hinting at Mrs. Hudson's fanatic fetish for my manhood? But we had been so discreet, so surely not.

'No. Nothing springs to mind, Holmes.'

'Really, Doctor? But as we are about to be squashed, surely this is the moment to ask me something that you have been meaning to ask me for ages and could not bring yourself to do it?'

Ah! He wasn't seeking a confession; he was showing off, as usual...

'Crikey, Holmes, now that you mention it, there was something. What was it? Ah, yes! Ready?'

'Yes, but at approximately thirty seconds before our oblivion, I shall have to ask you to hurry up...'

'Which school did you go to?'

Suddenly Holmes shot past me, as if he was swimming the crawl for England on the top of a rocket, and, as he passed me by, he shouted "Westminster!" He crashed into the wooden panels mended by the efficient Germans, ramming it like a billy goat! There was a terrific rendering of splintering wood as he disappeared through the wall. As the warm yellow light flooded in, I heard him shout out: "but it should have been Winchester!"

There was precious little space left between me and the ceiling, just a few inches, but I remembered my army training. I collapsed onto my side and threw my body into a roll, as fast as a hungry baby, but I struggled to re-arrange myself on arrival at the opening – I just couldn't find the room 'twixt floor and ceiling to lift myself up and climb over the newly-created threshold of splintered wood. I simply couldn't manage it! Then the ceiling touched my shoulder and pushed me down towards the floor. Then the pressure was on my back, forcing me downwards onto the metal plate. Then I could feel the cold iron forcing my spine into my back, harder and harder until it hurt so much that I was looking forward to hearing the snap of bones and it would all be over. Then, this was the end? Oh wouldn't it have been nice if I had had the time to... My body screamed in pain! Metal touched both sides of my head and I knew there was no escape now. My mind was swimming with terror, a swirl of blotchy black and red explosions. Then, in that last earthly moment, I heard Sherlock Holmes shout: "Take that, *fraulein*!" and I knew that he was safe and the world would be a better place for it. Somebody turned the lights off. I heard a woman's scream – such a desperately blood-curdling shriek it could only announce my entrance into Hell.

* * *

Prince Soltykoff's country residence was also in Sunningdale. As mentioned earlier by Mr. Hatherley, it was only just around the corner from where he found himself abandoned, and we had located that easily enough, all thanks to the ingenuity of Sherlock Holmes. When I asked him how he had found the location of the counterfeiters' lair, the great detective reminded me about the telegram he received at the railway station. It had been sent in response to his enquiry of even earlier

The great detective had a rather casual outlook upon our imminent death predicament.

that morning, which had been to Mr. John Phillips at the Oxford University Museum of Natural History. Apparently, he had published a paper: *The Geology of Oxford and the Valley of the Thames,* a few years ago. On it, he had marked the elements and minerals of southern England in great detail. The Sunningdale seam of fuller's earth was tiny, but even the smallest deposit showed up on Phillips's map, which was enough to identify the address. Once again, I marvelled at the scope of Sherlock Holmes's remarkable knowledge, not just limited to facts and figures but to everything else that is important in life; everything that surrounds us. He was able to make the connections from information he had accumulated and then produce it when needed, on demand, and this made him stand head and shoulders above any other detective.

When I came to, I was lying on a sofa with a rich, floral pattern, fully-dressed in my morning coat and with a fine blanket over me. I was in a very smart drawing room and not alone. My first recollection is hearing the voices of men nearby, all jolly and light, but my second is when my eyes fluttered open to the joyous sight of a very familiar face and a cup of tea clinking under my nose.

'Mrs. Hudson. You are a sight for sore eyes.' I knew now for certain that I was in this world rather than the next.

'As are you, Doctor Watson, now that you are awake,' whispered she, close up with her sweet, perfumed breath drifting across to me. 'Mister Holmes tells us that you were only a moment away from becoming a slice of luncheon-meat. Now, let me just check your legs...'

She slid her hand down my left leg. I lifted it. Then, she smiled and looked me in the eye as she moved her hand back up, stopped off *en-route* for an oh-so-subtle caress of my dickiedoodah – her preferred anatomy – and then slid down my right. I lifted that one successfully too.

'Good!' Mrs. Hudson leaned in close to my ear. 'I shall check on that more closely when we are not in company.' She pulled back again to give me more a sight of the room. This is when I noticed a group of gentlemen standing nearby, all clustered by a table. One was Prince Soltykoff and another was known better to me. He ambled over, glass in hand.

'Ah, there you are, Watson,' remarked Sherlock Holmes, whilst drawing heavily upon a Sobranie. 'I see that you have use of your legs. I am relieved because I wasn't sure if it was your spine that made the cracking noise or whether it was the German woman's front teeth being knocked out.'

'I am haunted by her deathly scream, Holmes! Please tell me that you did not have to treat her roughly. Well, not for my sakes...'

'I had precious little time, Doctor. There was the bicycle that the German wench was mounted upon?'

'How could I forget?'

'Instinctively, I levelled my walking stick with my shoulder, like a Masai warrior, and I launched it towards the rear wheel of the bicycle. *Tishi!* It jammed the wheel! The wench went over the handlebars, head-first, and planted her face into a metal toolbox. So, like you said, she started howling and screaming, like a banshee, but with no electricity the hydraulic press failed and you were delivered.'

'Thank you. Thank you very much, Holmes.'

'It is my pleasure. I am sorry your head has now taken the appearance of a forceps birth, but at least you still have one.'

'Stop it, Mister Holmes! No, John, you do not have such an appearance.'

I noticed Sherlock Holmes furrow his brows at the urgent familiarity in Mrs. Hudson's language. Luckily, we were saved an interrogation by a royal interruption.

'Charlotte, dear...' said the Prince, 'we are ready for you to sign. Bring the doctor with you.'

'Your highness,' said Holmes, all smarmy-like, 'as Doctor Watson is only just restored to us, may I offer my autograph services?'

'No, thank you, Mister Holmes. We require a man of professional qualification, a gentleman of good standing in the community, to witness of our Deed here and make it legally binding.'

I stood up and shook myself down. I gave Holmes a wink of my professionally qualified eye and presented myself at the table.

'May I introduce Mr. Edgar Cohen and Mr. Charles Harrod,' said the Prince. I shook the hand of each gentleman. 'For the sole purpose of your comfort in counter-signing this Deed, I shall inform you of its purpose. Mrs. Hudson and I are the mortgage holders of land and retail premises located on the Brompton Road in Knightsbridge.'

I glanced at Mrs. Hudson, eyes wide in surprise. She gave me her most impassive look, raised her head high and then turned away, clearly miffed and chuffed at the same time now that her secret life in business with Prince Soltykoff had been revealed. The minx! Holmes and I would never look on her as being our landlady and housekeeper in the same light ever again.

'Seven years ago,' continued the Prince, 'Mister Harrod suffered a fire that burned his shop to the ground. He has since re-constructed the building and refitted the shop with funds appropriated from this mortgage. Mister Cohen here is purchasing the shop's name and goodwill and the property title from Mister Harrod, thus allowing for repayment of the mortgage and releasing Mister Harrod from any obligation to the holders. You sign as witness, Doctor, just there...'

I looked at the document laid out on the table. I could see that the title holder was none other than Mrs. Charlotte Hudson! There was no mention of the Prince but I assumed that he was standing behind her, not wishing to have his royal name associated with any style of trade, money-lending in particular.

I was handed a fine fountain pen by Mr. Harrod. I had heard about his eponymous grocery store in Knightsbridge village but I had never visited. I told Mr. Harrod this.

'Then, in gratitude for your service to us all today, Doctor, I would like you to invite you for luncheon in our grocery store restaurant. After which, I shall be proud to show you around our modest shop. Would next Tuesday be suitable?'

'May I bring my friend, here?' And I pointed the pen at Sherlock Holmes.

'Ah, the infamous Mister Sherlock Holmes? Why, do you think that he would have time to join us?' I had to hand it to Mr. Harrod – he was one hell of an act and one could see why he had been such a successful tradesman. He turned around to face my companion and made a small bow.

'If you are able to join us, Mister Holmes, you shall be our guest of honour!'

Sherlock Holmes broke into his broadest and widest of smiles. 'I accept your *very kind* invitation, Mister Harrod…' Well, as we know, dear adventure-enthusiast, there was nothing like naked flattery to procure the undivided attention of Sherlock Holmes.

I signed on the line and everybody around me smiled and laughed, old Saltycock's walrus moustache waving up and down in time to his chortles. All I could think of was how lucky I was to be alive.

* * *

Once again, dear adventure-enthusiast, you deserve an epitaph to this extraordinary story. Naturally, the principal concern was whether we reached Ascot racecourse in time to back Gold in the Gold Cup. I am pleased to inform you that we did! We turned our one hundred guineas into seven. This was a fine outcome but a mere trifle of a sum when you consider that Bertie The Bounder cleared nearly two hundred thousand- he was last seen capering around the enclosure singing *Saltycock The Magnificent!* And there, nestled between the two princes, was the English rose Charlotte Hudson, beaming serenely from ear to ear and looking quite the Society princess.

As for Mr. Hatherley, we interrogated him on Saturday morning, just after we had taken our seats on the train to London. He told us how he sank into the heavy ground that ran down the side of the counterfeiters' property. He ended up stuck in the bog, right up to his chest. Inspector Bradstreet and Sergeant Jolyon answered his cries for help; they spent such a long time dragging him out of the mire that they missed the Germans and the Englishman making their escape out of the front door. All traces of the fugitives disappeared and, mysteriously, the house caught fire shortly afterwards. It burned to the ground. From that day to this no word has ever been heard either of the tongue-chewing Elise, the counterfeiting racehorse trainer, Colonel Blanders-Stark, or the morose Mr. Crackshot.

'Well, it has been a pretty business for me!' concluded the engineer. 'I have lost my tongue, albeit just the flicky tip but I shall talk with a lisp for the rest of my life. I have lost a fifty-guinea fee, and I am out of pocket for my costs. Last, but not least, I have lost my thumb. What have I gained?'

'Experience!' said Holmes, laughing. 'It may be of value in the future, you know, for you have only to put into words this tale of woe to gain reputation of being excellent company for the remainder of your existence. But you are incorrect on one point in the summary of your personal circumstances...'

Holmes extracted something small and pink from his coat pocket and held it up. 'I suggest you pickle this in a jam jar of alcohol.'

And with that advice he threw Mr. Hatherley his thumb!

All of us had a cheeky winner in the Gold Cup.